ANANSI

does the

IMPOSSIBLE!

To my son's wife, Adele Aardema,
who does many of my impossibles!
—V. A.

For Natalie and Brian
—L. D.

Anansi Does the Impossible! is retold from Verna Aardema's book, *The Sky God Stories*,
published by Coward-McCann, Inc., New York, 1960. That book is out of print, and the
rights have been returned to Mrs. Aardema.

The previous source is Robert S. Rattray's book, *Akan-Ahanti Folktales*, published by
Oxford, London, 1930. Captain Rattray died in 1939, so his books are in the public domain.

Atheneum Books for Young Readers
An imprint of Simon & Schuster Children's Publishing Division
1230 Avenue of the Americas
New York, New York 10020
Text copyright © 1997 by Verna Aardema
Illustrations copyright © 1997 by Lisa Desimini

Book design by Ann Bobco
The text of this book is set in Memphis Bold.
The art for this book was prepared with oil glazing, cut paper, and other materials.
The spiders were made out of black velvet paper.

Printed in the United States of America
First Edition
10 9 8 7 6 5 4 3 2 1

Library of Congress Cataloging-in-Publication Data
Aardema, Verna.
Anansi does the impossible! : an Ashanti tale / retold by Verna Aardema ;
illustrated by Lisa Desimini.—1st ed.
p. cm.
"An Anne Schwartz book."
Includes bibliographical references. (p.).
Summary: Anansi and his wife outsmart the Sky God and win back
the beloved folktales of their people.
ISBN 0-689-81092-X
1. Anansi (Legendary character)—Legends. [1. Anansi (Legendary character)—Legends.
2. Folklore—Africa, West.] I. Desimini, Lisa, ill. II. Title.
PZ8.1.A213Al   1997
398.2'0966'0452544—dc20
[E]   96-20033

ANANSI
does the
IMPOSSIBLE!
AN ASHANTI TALE

retold by
VERNA AARDEMA

illustrated by
LISA DESIMINI

AN ANNE SCHWARTZ BOOK
ATHENEUM BOOKS FOR YOUNG READERS

glossary

Anansi (Uh-NAHN-see): One of the names of the cunning spider who is the hero in many tales told by the indigenous peoples who live around the Gulf of Guinea

Ashanti (Uh-SHAHN-tee): The people of Ashantiland, which is located on the Gulf of Guinea and is now called Nigeria

Aso (AY-soh): Anansi's wife

fu-fu (foo-foo): Indicates that a fruit or vegetable is mashed, such as mashed banana or yam

ghe (ghay): Ideophone for laughter

goler (GOH-ler): Ideophone for the sound of water gurgling out of a bottle

k-pari (kuh-PAH-ree): The sound of an object being dragged over the ground

k-pong (kuh-PONG): Ideophone for a roundabout movement

kwo (k-woh): Ideophone expressing disgust

mimosa (me-MOH-suh): A leguminous tree having pink, yellow, or white flowers

odum (oh-DOOM): Ashanti name for a tree, possibly a native palm

pesa (PAY-suh): The breathy sound of whispering

RIM (REEM): Ideophone indicating a quick move

twe (tway): Ideophone for laughter

wasa-wusu (WAH-suh-WOO-soo): Ideophone for the motion of a crawling snake

WHEE (WHAY): The flashing of lightning

"When the earth was set down and the sky was lifted up": This reflects an ancient belief that the sky was once close to the earth. However, when people began to break off pieces of it and eat them, the creator, Nyame (En-YAH-may), lifted it high above their reach.

Long, long ago, when the earth was
set down and the sky was lifted up,
all folktales were owned by the Sky God.

One day, Anansi the Spider said to his wife, "Aso, it is wrong that the tales our storytellers have told for generations belong to the Sky God. I'm going to buy them for our earth people."

Aso said, "Do you really think you can bargain with anyone so powerful? Anansi, I fear you are taking a morsel too big to fit your mouth."

"Well, we shall see," said Anansi. And the very next day he went to the Sky God.

Puffing out his chest, he said, "Your Excellency, I have come to buy your stories."

The Sky God beat his thunder, *TUNN, TUNN, TUNN*. "Kwo!" he bellowed. "What makes you think you can buy them? Kings have tried and failed. And you are not even a man!"

"Wh-wh-what would you want in exchange for them?" asked Anansi.

The Sky God rubbed his great chin. At last he said, "The price is three impossible tasks. Bring me a live python, a real fairy, and forty-seven stinging hornets."

"I can manage that," said Anansi.

Then he hurried straight home to Aso.

Anansi told her, "I have to pay a live python, a real fairy, and forty-seven stinging hornets for the stories. However can I manage that?"

Aso thought and thought. Finally, she said, "I know how to begin." And she whispered, *pesa, pesa, pesa,* in Anansi's ear.

Anansi chuckled, *gug, gug, gug!* At once he ran with Aso to a nearby river. There they sat on a log and waited.

Presently, a python came slithering, *wasa-wusu*,
wasa-wusu, down to the water to drink.

Anansi said in a loud voice, "It is longer than he is."

"Not longer!" shouted Aso. "Maybe just as long.
But not *longer!*"

The big snake raised his head. "What are you two arguing about?" he asked.

"I say the log we're sitting on is longer than you are," Anansi answered. "But my wife says it is not."

"*Sss,*" hissed the python. "This small thing! I know I am longer. I *feel* longer."

"Well," said Anansi, "you *look* shorter to me."

"I'll show you," said the python. He lay down on the log, putting his nose even with one end of it.

"Your tail is too short," said Anansi. And *RIM,* he gave the tail a pull.

"Now my nose is too short," cried the python, and he wriggled back to the end of the log.

"I know what to do," said Aso. "Tie his tail to the other end. Then he can make himself longer."

Anansi took a long bush rope and began winding it around the snake's tail and the log, *k-pong, k-pong, k-pong.*

The python tried to make himself longer. He stretched and stretched, grunting, *unh, unh, unh.* Meanwhile, Anansi kept winding—until he'd wound the rope all the way up to the python's head.

When he had the snake tied tight, he cried,
"You foolish python! You let me catch you! Now
I'm going to take you to the Sky God." And off he
went, dragging the python behind him.

When Anansi gave the huge snake to the Sky God,
his scowl darkened the sun. He said, "It is true, you
have brought me the python. But you have yet to
bring a real fairy and forty-seven stinging hornets."

Anansi went home to Aso and asked, "How are we going to catch a fairy?"

Aso thought and thought. Finally, she said, "I know how!" And she whispered, *pesa, pesa, pesa,* to Anansi.

Anansi laughed, *twe, twe, twe!* As Aso had suggested, he carved a wooden fairy and covered it with sticky gum from a mimosa tree. Aso put a tiny dish of banana fu-fu into its hand.

When the moon was bright, Anansi took the make-believe fairy to the odum tree where the fairies liked to play. He tied a long string to the wooden fairy's back and another to its head. Then, clutching the ends of the strings, he hid behind some bushes.

Presently, some fairies came tripping to the odum tree. They danced around it, *lip, lip, lip.* And one of them cried in a tinkling voice, "Look! Here is a stranger! She has a dish of fu-fu."

The fairy's sister smacked her small lips, *puh, puh, puh.* "Ask her to give us some," she said.

So the first fairy asked, "Kind stranger, may I please have a taste of your fu-fu?"

Anansi pulled one string, and the doll nodded its head.

The fairy took a tiny taste. "Ooh," she said, "your fu-fu is delicious. Thank you."

The wooden fairy said nothing.

"Look," said the first fairy. "I told her *thank you*, yet she doesn't answer me."

"Slap her spanking place," said the sister.

The first fairy hit hard, *PA!* Her hand stuck. "Let me go! Let me go!" she cried.

The sister said, "Hit her again! That will teach her to let you go."

The first fairy struck the doll with her other hand, *PA!* And that stuck, too.

Quickly, Anansi pulled the strings. Now
the doll with the fairy attached came
bumping over to him, *k-pari, k-pari, k-pari.*
The little fairy screamed, eeee, in her
eerie little voice as she was being dragged
away—and her sisters shrieked, *EEE, EEE,*
EEEEE! as they ran after her.

Anansi soon outran those other fairies.
Then he said to the one he had caught,
"Little fairy, I'm going to take you to the Sky
God." And he did.

When the Sky God saw Anansi coming
with the fairy, he roared, "How can a
measly creature like you perform these
impossible tasks?" But then he added, "I
admit that the python and the fairy are
here. Still, you have not brought me the
forty-seven hornets."

Anansi ran home to Aso and asked, "How are we
going to catch forty-seven hornets?"
Aso thought and thought. Finally, she said, "I know
how!" And she whispered, *pesa, pesa, pesa,* to Anansi.
Anansi laughed, *ghe, ghe, ghe!*

As Aso had suggested, he plucked a bottle-shaped gourd from a calabash tree, whittled a wooden cork for it, and filled it with water from the river. Next, he found a hornet's nest in a bush. Climbing high up a nearby tree, he tipped the bottle and let the water gurgle, *goler, goler, goler,* down upon the hornets.

"My brothers," called Anansi, "do you
want a better shelter? See, in this calabash
you will be safe and dry." He held out the
empty gourd.

The hornets buzzed around it. One flew in,
then another, and another. When Anansi had
counted forty-seven of them, he popped the
stopper in, *KOP!* "Little hornets," he said,
"I'm going to take you to the Sky God." And
off he went.

The Sky God saw Anansi coming. At once, he flashed his lightning, *WHEE, WHEE, WHEE,* and beat his thunder, *TUNN, TUNN, TUNN.*

Holding out the buzzing gourd, Anansi said, "In here are the forty-seven stinging hornets. Do you want to count them?"

"No!" cried the Sky God. He threw up his hands in resignation and said, "Anansi, you have paid the price—the live python, the real fairy, and the forty-seven stinging hornets are mine. From now on, the stories belong to you."

Anansi thanked the Sky God. Then he hurried home.

That night, the people of the village gathered inside
a circle of fires for storytelling. And Anansi told how he
and Aso had managed to buy the Sky God Stories.
The people rejoiced, chanting:

"Honor to Anansi!

"Honor to Aso!

"Honor to Anansi and Aso!"

And from that day to this, the folk stories of West Africa
have been called Anansi Tales.